Copyright © 2023 – Leroy Davis.

About the Author

Leroy Davis Jr. is an author from Norwalk CT - born and raised. He graduated from high school, did some college with art. The reason why he wrote this book is in honor for his kids and their future. His kids are the reason and inspiration behind this creative art piece. This was a long journey that he took head-on with all the stories he has created. He has been writing since 2017 & he came up with his story while he was at his worst. That is until he found his way. GOD heard him and whispered to him, and that is when he took his gift with his kids by his side and started writing. Today he stands as an author, with stories that will continue now and forever.

M.U.S.

Magnificent Coming Series #1 is powered by: Magnificent Universal Squad Comic's

Owner/Creator: Leroy Davis Jr

Illustrated by: SELENIKE

==

How did Ana'-De-Luna get her powers?

Ana'-De-Luna gets her powers by the red moon. This moon was a dark bloody red moon. This red moon started to drain out rain drops that had red bugs inside of them. The bugs crawled all over her until one magically puncture its way through her skin. This bug made its way to her heart and changed it into the red moon. Now her heart and the medallion crescent around her neck generates the power from the medallion to her heart within her. The infamous powers of the red moon gave her strength and beyond.

ON THAT NIGHT OCT 30, SHE BECAME THE PRINCESS OF THE RED MOON.

The story begins with Ana'-De-Luna sleeping in her abandoned home. While she's sleeping, the bad dream has just begun. And thus Leroy Davis Jr's story begins.

"THE YEAR WAS 2015, THE TIME WAS 9 PM AND THE DATE WAS OCTOBER 30. THERE WAS A BLOODY FULL RED MOON AND ON THIS NIGHT THERE WAS A VIGILANTE PRINCESS OF THE NIGHT WHO ONLY WAKES UP AT THE STROKE OF 9PM. SHE WAS THE SHADOW OF THE NIGHT, NO ONE KNEW WHO SHE WAS OR WHAT SHE WAS UP TO. ALL WE KNOW IS IT WAS THE NIGHT OF ALL NIGHTS. SHE APPEARS ONLY AT NIGHT AND SHE ALWAYS FIGHTS THROUGH THE NIGHT, BATTLING BAD GUYS AND WOMEN THROUGH THE DARKNESS. BUT SOMETHING STRANGE HAPPENED ON THIS NIGHT, SOMETHING CAME OUT OF THE RED MOON.
A WOMAN FIGURE APPEARS IN THE AIR AND THEN HOVERS UP IN THE RED SKY. IT WAS A DARK, DARK SKY. THE MOON GLAZED THE SKY WITH SHADES OF RED.

THIS WOMAN IS NOW IN VIEW AND SEES THE SLEEPING PRINCESS. THE WOMAN SPEAKS FROM HER MIND TO THE PRINCESS IN HER DREAM STATE... "IT'S TIME TO MAKE A GRAND ENTRANCE MY VIGILANTE PRINCESS; TO MAKE US PROUD AND BRING DOWN THOSE BAD MEN AND WOMEN. THEY BRING MADNESS TO CRIMSON IN THE DARKNESS OF THE NIGHT. YOU ARE THE CHOSEN ONE."
WHISPERING. "YOU'RE THE CHOSEN ONE. YOU'RE THE CHOSEN ONE."
"GO FORTH MY VIGILANTE PRINCESS, WHERE ALL BAD THINGS HAPPEN DURING THE NIGHT IN THE CITY OF CRIMSON. I AM JASMINE- WAKE UP MY VIGILANTE PRINCESS. WAKE UP. WAKE UP."
ANA: WHAT A DREAM! YAWNING.

WE SEE AN-DE LUNA, CLIMBING OUT OF THE WINDOW. CUT TO HER SITTING ON TOP OF A BUILDING,
SHE'S LISTENING TO MUSIC, COLORING A PICTURE WITH CRAYONS AND IS SINGING ALONG TO MUSIC IN HER EAR BUDS.
THEN THE MUSIC STOPS, SHE PUTS HER HEAD UP AND LOOKS AROUND, (WE SEE THE PICTURE SHE'S DRAWING IT'S THE IMAGE OF THE LADY IN HER DREAMS. SHE LOOKS STRAIGHT AT THE CAMERA AND SPEAKS)
"LOOKS LIKE A NOT-SO-LONG NIGHT AHEAD? THE STREETS OF CRIMSON ARE SO DELIGHTFUL TONIGHT; I CAN SEE THE ENTIRE CITY FROM UP HERE. I DON'T SEE MUCH GOING ON TONIGHT. I'VE BEEN SITTING HERE WAITING FOR SOME TROUBLE TO STIR UP. (KICKS HER FOOT UP IN THE AIR, FRUSTRATED) I REMEMBER MY DREAM, I HAD AND IT'S STILL ON MY MIND. SEE I DREW HER, THE WAY SHE WAS IN MY DREAM. WHAT DOES SHE WANT? DON'T LAUGH I'M NOT THE BEST DRAWER, BUT I KNOW WHO IS THE BEST DRAWER...HE CREATED ME! I CAN GIVE YOU A HINT HIS NAME IS... (.WHISPERING) LEROY"

WIDOW WHYTE: I SEE YOU VIGILANTE PRINCESS OF THE NIGHT, I'M WATCHING OUT FOR YOU. I WONDER WHAT SHE'S UP TO TONIGHT. IT'S 9 PM AND SHE'S AT IT AGAIN. WHAT IS SHE LOOKING AT, ANYTHING IN PARTICULAR?
LET ME VIEW THIS WITH MY BINOCULARS. HMMM...A BOOK, A PICTURE? WAIT, WHAT'S THIS, A WAREHOUSE HEIST; THEY'RE CLEANING OUT THE PLACE AND PUTTING THE MERCHANDISE IN THOSE TRUCKS? OH NO, SHE'S ON THE MOVE!
ANA-DE LUNA-HUH? WAIT I HEAR SOMETHING OR SOMEONE!
(NARRATOR) AFTER HEARING THE CHATTING IN THE DISTANCE, SHE LEAPS UP AND JUMPS DOWN TO THE NEXT LEVEL OF THE BUILDING. (CHATTING IN THE DISTANCE)

MAN'S VOICE- EVERYONE, THIS WILL NOT BE EASY BUT WE HAVE TO CLEAR THIS WAREHOUSE, COMPLETELY. WE HAVE TO LOAD ALL THE MERCHANDISE INTO THESE 4 TRUCKS.
(ANA-DE-LUNA WALKS AROUND THE BUILDING NOT KNOWING WHERE THE VOICE IS COMING FROM)
ANA-DE-LUNA- WHERE COULD THIS BE? THERE THEY ARE, WAIT WHAT ARE THEY'RE DOING?
(ANA-DE-LUNA GETS A LITTLE CLOSER AND LISTENS IN ON THE CONVERSATION
MAN VOICE 2#- WE NEED MORE GUYS, MORE MORE GUYS, MORE GUYS. IT'S TAKING TOO LONG AND TIME IS WASTING.
MAN'S VOICE#1- WE WILL BE OKAY, THE ALARMS ARE DISABLED. WE ARE THE ONLY ONES OUT HERE, WHO'S UP AT 9PM?
PHONE RINGS
BIG BOSS- (YELLING) HURRY UP YOU MORONS. I NEED ALL THE MERCHANDISE LOADED INTO THE TRUCKS. I'VE ALREADY SENT BANK ROBBERS #1 AND #2 TO THE CRIMSON BANK OF CRIMSONTOWN. I NEED EVERYTHING TO GO AS PLANNED SO DON'T Y'ALL FAIL ME.!!!!

(Narrator)
(Ana-De Luna goes to the end of the building)
♪♪ -click...
(Narrator)
(Walkman music playing, so we can hear) Ana toon to these lyrics...
Come Miss Ana, Ana-De-Luna, daylight comes and she wants to go home.
Man's Voice#1- Ok boss. We we'll be finished soon. The night is young the moon is bloody red!
(Music Echoes Out)
(Ana-De-Luna sees men robbing a warehouse nearby.)
Thinking to herself..." look what we have here! When I thought it was going to be an easy night. I guess it's showtime! Hold up I have to be cautious and not be seen by those bad guys."

WIDOW WHYTE -OK, THERE SHE GOES!
(NARRATOR)
(ANA-DE-LUNA LEAPS FROM THE BUILDING ON TO THE NEXT BUILDING AND WORKS HER WAY TO THE GROUND...)
WIDOW WHYTE I HAVE TO SEE THIS UP CLOSE AND PERSONAL.
ANOTHER LEAP
NARRATOR (...AND LANDS FEET FIRST, STEADIES HERSELF AND STEALTHLY SNEAKS FORWARD)

NARRATOR: WE HEAR 2 GUYS ON THE PHONE. (BOTH GRUNTS SOFTLY)
KA-POOOOW
ANA-DE-LUNA GOT YOU (SHHHH) MUSTN'T BE HEARD (SHE WHISPER)!
(2MEN GOES DOWN)
POOOW!
CRASH!
CRAAAACK
SMAAAASH!
(ANA-DE-LUNA LEAPS OVER TO WHERE THESE GUYS ARE STANDING AND PROCEEDS TO SMASH THEM UP IN AN INSTANT AND AUTOMATICALLY DEMOLISHES TWO MORE THAT LUNGE AT HER.)
ANA-DE-LUNA THIS IS EASIER THAN I THOUGHT IT WOULD BE.
POOW!
CRASH
CROOCKH
(NARRATOR)(ANA-DE-LUNA TAKES OUT A FEW MORE,(FOR MORE FUN))

KA-POOOWWW
GRAAAASH
POOOWWWW
ANA-DE-LUNA 10 MEN DOWN, I GUESS I'M ON A ROLL? YES I AM!
SBAAAM!!
(Narrator)
ANA-DE-LUNA THOUGHT SHE HAD THE UPPER HAND, BUT SHE DIDN'T SEE THE OTHER TWO MEN (WHO GRABBED HER)
ANA-DE-LUNA
CRAP I GUESS I SHOULD'T CELEBRATE NOW.
AH!
STUD!!

CRIMSON SOLDIER: WHO ARE YOU?!
ANA-DE-LUNA: OK TAKE IT EASY, DON'T HURT ME!
ANA-DE-LUNA: TAKE IT EASY, THAT'S WAY TO TIGHT
CRIMSON SOLDIER: I SAID, WHO ARE YOU? ANSWER ME NOW!
ANA-DE-LUNA: OK CALM DOWN SIR. LET'S SAY YOU LET ME GO AND PRETEND I WASN'T HERE.
CRIMSON SOLDIER- DO I LOOK CALM? DO I? THAT IS NOT AN OPTION FOR YOU WHOEVER YOU ARE!

ANA-DE-LUNA:
LISTEN, IF YOU DO KEEP ME I'M NOT SAYING A WORD TO YOU GUYS!

CRIMSON SOLDIER:
WHO ARE YOU? WHY ARE YOU HERE? DON'T LET ME SAY IT AGAIN!, ANSWER ME! YOU CAN STAY SILENT BUT THE BOSS AIN'T GONNA LIKE IT AND HE WILL KILL YOU!

(CRIMSON SOLDIER: GETS ON THE WALKIE TALKIE)

HEY BOSS WE'VE FOUND AN INTRUDER ON THE SITE!

MAN VOICE #1 :
WE'LL BE RIGHT THERE, HOLD THEM
DOWN UNTIL WE GET THERE.
MAN VOICE #2:
(YELLING AT MAN
VOICE#1) YOU
SAID NO ONE
ELSE WAS
HERE, NO ONE ,
ON ONE ELSE
WAS HERE!
LOOK, THEY
FOUND SOMEONE!
CRIMSON SOLDIER:
BOSS WE SEEN
HER, SHE'S BEEN
ALL OVER THE
WAREHOUSE
BEATING UP OUR
MEN. SEEMS LIKE
SHE'S TAKEN OUT
10 OF US!
ANA-DE-LUNA :
WAIT 10,
THAT'S A LIE!

MAN'S VOICE#1: SO YOU TOOK OUT SOME OF MY MEN?! THEY SAID ABOUT 20, A GIRL LIKE YOU MUST BE PRETTY TOUGH TO MANHANDLE THAT MANY SOLDIERS.
ANA-DE-LUNA: NO THEY'RE LYING! THEY WE'RE KNOCKED OUT WAY BEFORE I GOT TO THEM. I GUESS THEY WERE SLEEPING ON THE JOB. OH, AND BY THE WAY, IT WAS ONLY 8 THAT WERE SLEEPING. I MEAN DO I LOOK TOUGH ENOUGH TO DO THAT TO 20 MEN?
MAN VOICE#2: I CAN'T SEE HER FACE. HER HOOD IS COVERING HER EYES. I DON'T KNOW ABOUT HER SHE SOUNDS STRONG. I CAN FEEL IT. YOU KNOW I SENSE IT.
WIDOW WHYTE: (WHISPERS) COME ON PICK UP!
ANA-DE-LUNA: MAYBE YOU SHOULD LISTEN TO YOUR PARTNER. I COULD BE VERY STRONG. I COULD BE VERY POWERFUL AND I MIGHT BE ABLE TO TAKE EACH AND EVERYONE OF YOU, OUT. YOU DID SAY I SEEM TOUGH CAUSE I SUPPOSEDLY, TOOK OUT A FEW SOLDIERS.
MAN VOICE#2: WELL SPOKEN, MAY I SAY LITTLE GIRL OR WOMAN, IT DOESN'T MATTER. SO MY PARTNER THINKS YOU ARE SUPER STRONG AND YOU TOOK OUT MY SOLDIERS, WHO WERE SUPPOSEDLY SLEEPING. LET'S FORGET ABOUT THAT FOR NOW. ANSWER ME THIS, WHO DO YOU WORK FOR?

(NARRATOR :
MEN ARE LAUGHING)
MAN VOICE 1#:
WE WILL SEE. WE ARE GIVING YOU A
CHANCE TO TELL US WHO YOU WORK
FOR
ANA-DE-LUNA:
MYSELF
WHYTE WIDOW:
THIS DOESN'T LOOK
GOOD FOR HER AT
ALL, DAMN BAD
SERVICE.
BIANCA:
I JUS GOT A CALL FROM WIDOW
WHYTE, BUT I COULDN'T HEAR
HER. EITHER THE CALL
DROPPED OR SOMEONE
DISCONNECTED US.
JEANNETTE:
THAT'S STRANGE GETTING A CALL FROM
HER PHONE AND BEING DISCONNECTED
LIKE THAT!
LEAH:
LET ME SEE IF I CAN
TRACK HER PHONE
FROM HERE ON MY
LAPTOP.
ANA-DE-LUNA:
LIKE I SAID, I WORK
FOR NO ONE BUT
MYSELF.
MAN 1#:
OK WE'LL SEE,
LET'S SEE WHAT
MY BOSS SAYS,
NOW YOU ARE
REALLY IN DEEP
TROUBLE.
ANA-DE-LUNA:
I AM REALLY
SCARED, I'M SHAKIN
IN MY BOOTS.

NARRATOR:(GETS ON CELL PHONE)
LEROY:HEY? ...
WIDOW WHYTE: DAMN THERE'S NO SERVICE OUT HERE AT ALL... WHY'S THAT GUY STANDING THERE FOR, HE'S CREEPING ME OUT?
LEROY: HEY EXCUSE ME? I DON'T MEAN TO BOTHER YOU..., BUT DO YOU KNOW THAT VIGILANTE ONLY COME OUT AT NIGHT? THEY FIGHT IN THE DARKENESS TO HIDE THEIR IDENTITY.
WIDOW WHYTE: SO WHO CARES, GET AMWAY FROM ME NOW!
MAN#1: "HEY BOSS, WE HAVE AN INTRUDER ON SITE!...SHE'S BEEN TAKING OUT SOME OF OUR MEN "
BOSS MAN: WHAT? WHY ARE YOU TELLING ME THIS? YOU KNOW WHAT TO DO DISPOSE OF WHOEVER THEY ARE! TAKE THEM OUT,AND GET MY MERCHANDISE TO ME,NOW! IF IT'S NOT DONE IMMEDIATELY,I WILL KILL BOTH OF YOU WITH MY BARE HANDS! YOU'VE CLEARLY BEEN TESTING WITH MY PATIENCE...STOP PLAYING AROUND AND GET THE JOB DONE.
BAAAM

MAN#1: WHAT SHOULD WE DO ABOUT THE INTRUDER AGAIN?
BOSS MAN: ARE YOU DUMB OR JUST PLAIN STUPID. I SAID DISPOSE OF HER!!!!
MAN VOICE#2: YOU ,YOU HEARD THE BOSS. DISPOSE OF HER,DISPOSE OF HER, DISPOSE OF HER!!!
(ANA-DE-LUNA: LAUGHS OUT LOUD)
SMAAACKKK
AH AH AH!!!
VOICE MAN#1: YOU THINK THIS IS FUNNY, HUH?
(MAN#1: SMACKS ANA-DE-LUNA).
(MAN#2: KNOCKS ANA -DE-LUNA DOWN WHILE IN THE CHAIR)
SBAAAM
SBAMMM
GRRR
ANA-DE-LUNA: GRUNTS
NARRATOR: ANA-DE-LUNA FALLS HARD,THAT THE ROPE SNAP.
ANA-DE-LUNA:YOUR GOING TO PAY FOR THAT!

WIDOW WHYTE: (FRUSTRATED!) SKYLAR! HELLO UGH!! I LOST VIDEO CONNECTION WITH SKYLAR. I CAN'T GET ANY SERVICE OUT HERE AT ALL, I NEED TO GET IN CONTACT WITH HEADQUARTES AND FAST.
NARRATOR: (WIDOW WHYTE GETS AMBUSHES BY 3 MYSTERIOUS WOMEN, ONE OF THEM GRABS WIDOW WHYTE AND SHE DROPS HER PHONE.)
WIDOW WHYTE: HEY UGH!!! I JUST GOT THAT PHONE.
SBAAAAM!
POWWW!!!
CRRRACK
SBAM!
MAN #1: HUSH, I'LL DEAL WITH IT THE WAY MY BRAIN IS TELLING ME. IT'S TELLING ME, "WHAT ARE YOU GOING TO DO ?" YOU'RE ALL ALONE LITTLE GIRL AND GUESS WHAT NO ONES AROUND HERE TO HEAR YOU SCREAM. ARE YOU READY FOR YOU DEATH?
CRRRACK
MAN #2: WHAT ARE YOU PREPARED TO DO ABOUT IT, ABOUT IT?

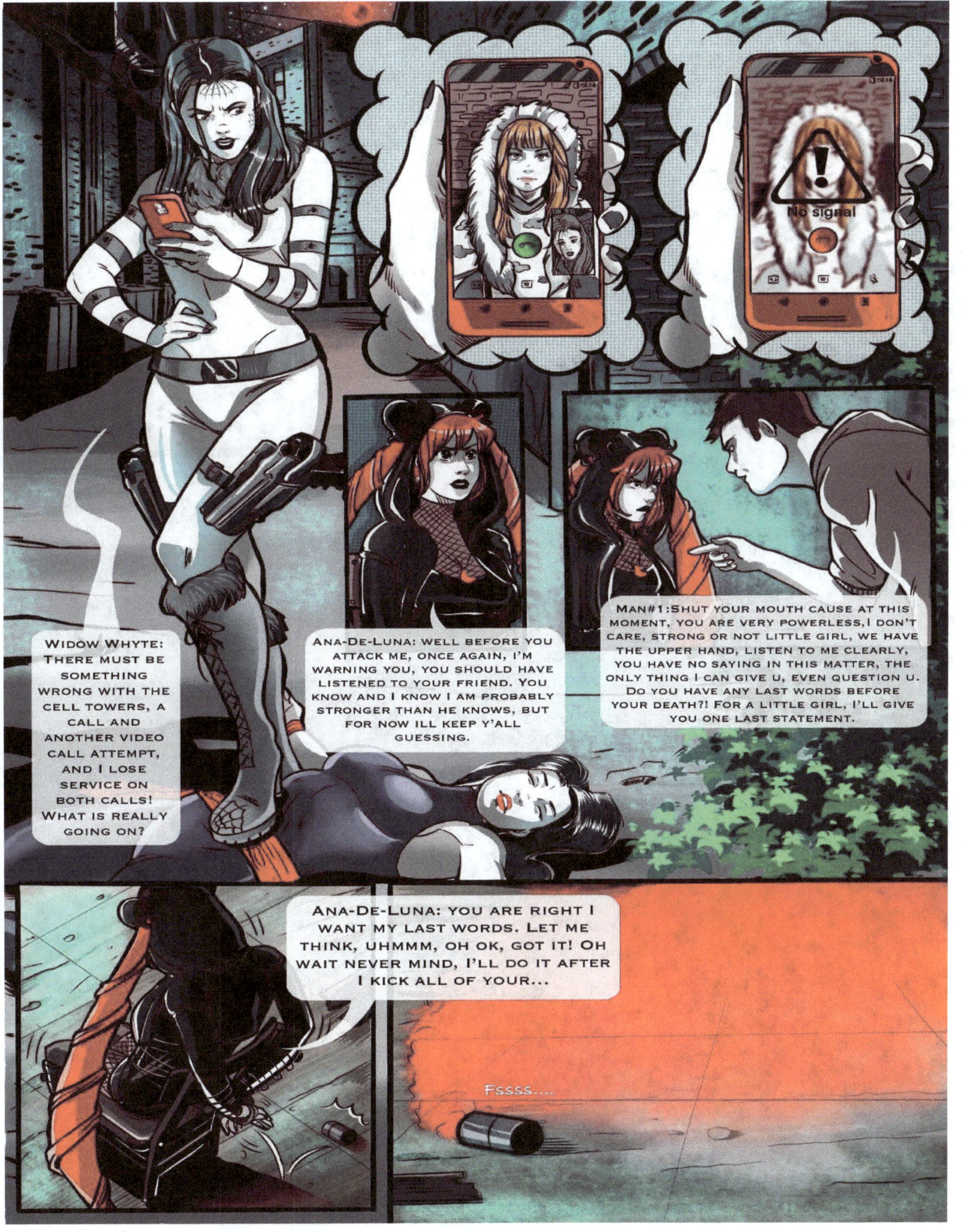

No signal
WIDOW WHYTE: THERE MUST BE SOMETHING WRONG WITH THE CELL TOWERS, A CALL AND ANOTHER VIDEO CALL ATTEMPT, AND I LOSE SERVICE ON BOTH CALLS! WHAT IS REALLY GOING ON?
ANA-DE-LUNA: WELL BEFORE YOU ATTACK ME, ONCE AGAIN, I'M WARNING YOU, YOU SHOULD HAVE LISTENED TO YOUR FRIEND. YOU KNOW AND I KNOW I AM PROBABLY STRONGER THAN HE KNOWS, BUT FOR NOW ILL KEEP Y'ALL GUESSING.
MAN#1:SHUT YOUR MOUTH CAUSE AT THIS MOMENT, YOU ARE VERY POWERLESS, I DON'T CARE, STRONG OR NOT LITTLE GIRL, WE HAVE THE UPPER HAND, LISTEN TO ME CLEARLY, YOU HAVE NO SAYING IN THIS MATTER, THE ONLY THING I CAN GIVE U, EVEN QUESTION U. DO YOU HAVE ANY LAST WORDS BEFORE YOUR DEATH?! FOR A LITTLE GIRL, I'LL GIVE YOU ONE LAST STATEMENT.
ANA-DE-LUNA: YOU ARE RIGHT I WANT MY LAST WORDS. LET ME THINK, UHMMM, OH OK, GOT IT! OH WAIT NEVER MIND, I'LL DO IT AFTER I KICK ALL OF YOUR...
FSSSS....

WIDOW WHYTE: WHAT A MINUTE.
WIDOW WHYTE: I SEE AN OPEN WINDOW IN THAT OFFICE BUILDING, MAYBE THERE'S A COMPUTER OR...FAX MACHINE IN THERE? I CAN SEND INFORMATION TO HEADQUARTERS'S!
WIDOW WHYTE: I GUESS THE ONLY WAY TO FIND OUT IS TO CLIMB UP TO THAT WINDOW, HERE I GO!
WIDOW WHYTE: (EXHAUSTED) THAT WAS EASIER THAN I THOUGHT!
WIDOW WHYTE: THAT WAS EASY.
WIDOW WHYTE: JACKPOT! JUST WHAT I WAS LOOKING FOR, LOTS OF COMPUTERS AND FAX MACHINES!
NARRATOR: WIDOW WHYTE FINDS A OFFICE FILLED WITH COMPUTER AND FAX MACHINE'S.
WIDOW WHYTE: (LOOKS THOUGH HER BINOCULARS) ..LOOK WHAT WE HAVE HERE, THEY SABOTAGED THE CELL TOWER. THAT'S WHY I DIDN'T HAVE ANY CELL SERVICE. THEY MUST HAVE SOME TECHNOLOGY IN PLACE FOR THEM TO USE THEIR OWN PHONES... I KNOW NOW SOMETHING REALLY GOING ON HERE. I WILL FIND OUT ABOUT THIS HEIST, AND I WILL FIND OUT WHO'S BEHIND THIS.

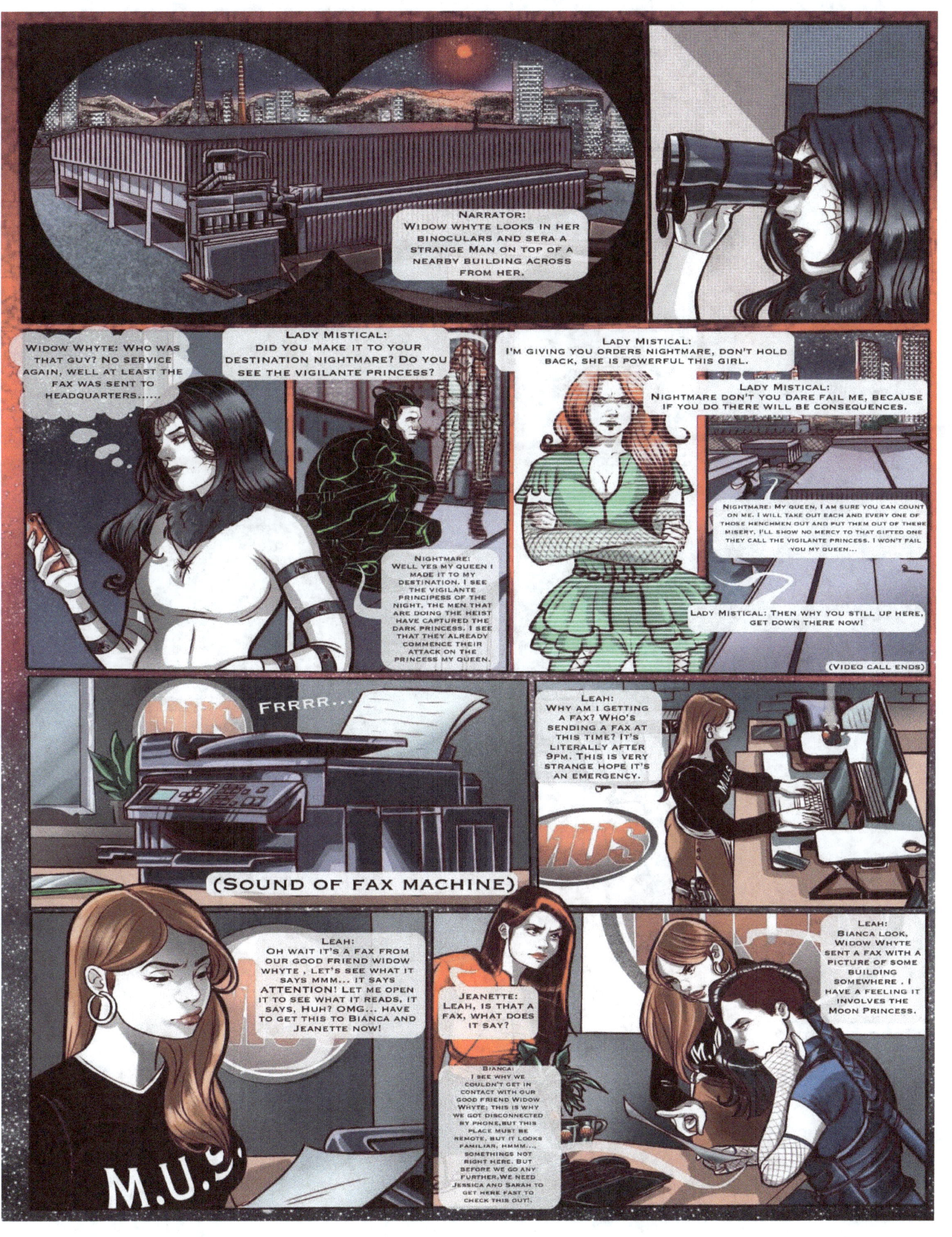

NARRATOR:
WIDOW WHYTE LOOKS IN HER BINOCULARS AND SERA A STRANGE MAN ON TOP OF A NEARBY BUILDING ACROSS FROM HER.
WIDOW WHYTE: WHO WAS THAT GUY? NO SERVICE AGAIN, WELL AT LEAST THE FAX WAS SENT TO HEADQUARTERS......
LADY MISTICAL:
DID YOU MAKE IT TO YOUR DESTINATION NIGHTMARE? DO YOU SEE THE VIGILANTE PRINCESS?
LADY MISTICAL:
I'M GIVING YOU ORDERS NIGHTMARE, DON'T HOLD BACK, SHE IS POWERFUL THIS GIRL.
LADY MISTICAL:
NIGHTMARE DON'T YOU DARE FAIL ME, BECAUSE IF YOU DO THERE WILL BE CONSEQUENCES.
NIGHTMARE:
WELL YES MY QUEEN I MADE IT TO MY DESTINATION. I SEE THE VIGILANTE PRINCIPESS OF THE NIGHT, THE MEN THAT ARE DOING THE HEIST HAVE CAPTURED THE DARK PRINCESS. I SEE THAT THEY ALREADY COMMENCE THEIR ATTACK ON THE PRINCESS MY QUEEN.
NIGHTMARE: MY QUEEN, I AM SURE YOU CAN COUNT ON ME. I WILL TAKE OUT EACH AND EVERY ONE OF THOSE HENCHMEN OUT AND PUT THEM OUT OF THERE MISERY. I'LL SHOW NO MERCY TO THAT GIFTED ONE THEY CALL THE VIGILANTE PRINCESS. I WON'T FAIL YOU MY QUEEN...
LADY MISTICAL: THEN WHY YOU STILL UP HERE, GET DOWN THERE NOW!
(VIDEO CALL ENDS)
FRRRR...
MUS
(SOUND OF FAX MACHINE)
LEAH:
WHY AM I GETTING A FAX? WHO'S SENDING A FAX AT THIS TIME? IT'S LITERALLY AFTER 9PM. THIS IS VERY STRANGE HOPE IT'S AN EMERGENCY.
LEAH:
OH WAIT IT'S A FAX FROM OUR GOOD FRIEND WIDOW WHYTE , LET'S SEE WHAT IT SAYS MMM... IT SAYS ATTENTION! LET ME OPEN IT TO SEE WHAT IT READS, IT SAYS, HUH? OMG... HAVE TO GET THIS TO BIANCA AND JEANETTE NOW!
JEANETTE:
LEAH, IS THAT A FAX, WHAT DOES IT SAY?
LEAH:
BIANCA LOOK, WIDOW WHYTE SENT A FAX WITH A PICTURE OF SOME BUILDING SOMEWHERE . I HAVE A FEELING IT INVOLVES THE MOON PRINCESS.
BIANCA:
I SEE WHY WE COULDN'T GET IN CONTACT WITH OUR GOOD FRIEND WIDOW WHYTE; THIS IS WHY WE GOT DISCONNECTED BY PHONE, BUT THIS PLACE MUST BE REMOTE, BUT IT LOOKS FAMILIAR, HMMM..., SOMETHINGS NOT RIGHT HERE. BUT BEFORE WE GO ANY FURTHER, WE NEED JESSICA AND SARAH TO GET HERE FAST TO CHECK THIS OUT!.
M.U.S.

MUS
Attention !
MUS
TO BE CONTINUED...

📷 magnificentuniversalsquad_365

▶️ M.U.S_25 Leroy Squad Davis Jr

🐦 Leroy_SQ

👻 Magnificent+2021

♪ themanleroy

🎮 TheManleroydee